LIMINAL MONSTER

ALSO BY LUKE TARZIAN

THE SHADOW TWINS SERIES

Vultures

House of Muir

ADJACENT MONSTERS

The World Maker Parable

The World Breaker Requiem

The World Reaper Odyssey

WHIMSY HELL

A Cup of Tea at the Mouth of Hell

Liminal Monster

ANTHOLOGIES

Dark Ends

Liminal Monster

Luke Tarzian

For every part of me I tried, and failed, to write.
I'm sorry.

PRELUDE
O, SORROW

A woman sits in a decrepit rocking chair atop the highest peak of a city so long-dead its name is but a dream. In one hand she holds a tattered silk-wrought mask; in the other, a needle and thread. Beyond her, beside her, behind her, encompassing the whole of the balcony, is the corpse of a *thing*. Even in death its eldritch grin persists, procuring screams from falling stars and sowing *pleasure* 'cross the moonlit streets of the city.

Sorrow stands at the precipice, back to the balustrade beneath which churns a cacophonous sea that smells of rot and piss and fear.

"Metaphors are peculiar," says the woman. "It is the choice of words, I think. You and I know well there is no 'sea,' and yet its use arouses chaos, illustrates the frantic ebb and flow of our decline presented as a million dying screams."

She looks up, scrutinizing Sorrow with orange eyes inside of which eternity drifts. Constellations and the gossamer web of galaxies dead and gone. She beckons Sorrow and the Chronicler of Ends obeys.

Sorrow kneels before the woman and observes.

"A needle and thread are perhaps the finest simulacra of Proprium's quill and ink, the means by which reality is writ."

The woman shifts her needle-wielding hand. Palm upturned, the implement takes flight, hovering before her like a sunlit shard of glass. The milk-white thread falls from the needle's eye and waits. Frayed and weightless, aimless and adrift; ink bereft of quill.

"From one, many," says the woman, and her words enchant the simulacra. Through the eye frayed thread is drawn; around the eye the loose ends deviate, reaching outward like the roots of trees. Desperate. Grasping.

"And from many, one." With her thumb and index finger, the woman mends the tarnished thread—but Sorrow still fixates on the needle's eye.

March 16, 2011

What is it about cemeteries that they offer such solace from the uncertainty of life, the chaos of reality?

This is a question I have asked myself a thousand times in the years since I last knelt before your grave.

I digress; we are fourteen years in the past, and the chaos of my life is yet to fully manifest, to rear its ugly head and leave me wandering like wind-swept virgin ash in the wake of all-consuming fire.

I kneel before your headstone. You are almost four months gone; my heart is a gaping wound. The winter sky is mottled grey; the clouds share in my grief.

I come asking questions about a girl, because I'm lost and the advice I need is kept behind the lips of a dead boy taken far before his time.

"She cheated on me."

"Fuck her."

"I'm lonely."

"Do you, buddy."

It's funny how prophetic imaginary conversations with the dead can be. No, not funny—ironic. Beautifully, agonizingly, ironic.

I stand and walk to my car. The dead can only offer so much hope and I can feel the sunset drinking of my sense with every rattling of the leaves.

WHEN SORROW WAKES, he sits atop a horse-drawn carriage. Beside him sits a man in black. From his face protrudes a raven's beak; atop his head sits a hat as tall as Sorrow's arm is long.

The night smells of distant rain.

A shriek annihilates the silence.

The carriage driver snaps his beak.

"Welcome to Own. May God have mercy on your soul."

Act I: A Song of Leaves

Leaves & Ash

April 8, 2014

*"In the center of the forest sits a house of leaves and ash.
Inside the house, his heart and lies."*

Where do you start the story of your life when its origin is constantly in flux? Gene Wolfe once said you never really learn how to write a novel; you simply learn how to write the novel your working on.

I wonder if that sentiment is applicable to life. Say it is. Pretend this all starts at *the end*. Pretend, for a moment, our story, my story—*this* story—starts April 8, 2014 in a fog of scotch and starlight as I rouse in a puddle of mud and self-wrought sick in a forest fucking dark. *Pretend*. Embarrassing, yes, but surely you'll forgive a man who only earlier in the day learned his two-years-dead ex-girlfriend is, in fact, *alive.*

(So many divergent threads.)

I stand and the odor of vomit clinging to my shirt is strong enough to make me retch and falsely swear I'll never drink again because, my god, I feel like *shit.*

"...Fuck...*y...ou.*"

Our brief and volatile time together blinks across my memory like a bout of salsa shits, abhorrent and summoning the urge to utter every curse word in my bag. I loved you; I hate you.

The darkness chuckles and I piss my pants.

"If only you knew."

I lean against a tree; it is hard to breathe. Reality and emotion are a muscle, a serpent wrapped around my neck.

"Relent," the darkness urges. *"Relent and you will see. You deserve to be free from the cruelty of this place. Why bend to atrocious things when you could leash them all? Relent!"*

Asphyxia takes me. She is gentle.

The forest giggles.

Inside a house there is a lake at the center of which an island sits. Upon the island, a spire of stone the color of virgin snow. Surrounding the tower, an orchard of memories. Echoes of misery and mirth entombed in the sour apples of Self.

Dry leaves fall like a gentle snow.

Self opens a journal of godskin. They chronicle the death of another world. How many times must this cycle repeat? When will they finally get it right?

(*"When might I finally be free?"*)

A cold wind encircles the island. It whispers to Self and the words are a dagger sheathed in their heart.

They touch their quill to the journal's parchment flesh and scrawl their sorrow 'til the wind no longer whispers and their heart is numb. Words have power.

In this hour, on this night of screaming knives, is my love for you renounced.

These will foster life.

They will end a thousand worlds.

Dreams. What strange, horrifying things.

I rouse against a tree. The world is grey; the

leaves are red. My mouth is dry and my skull is pounding with the force of a fucking Christmas solicitor.

Breathe.

Congestion. Hungover.

At least my clothes are clean.

Check my phone. April 8, 2014. Half six a.m..

I stand; I'm stiff. I walk, aimless.

The crows are awake. They speak of a house. I know because of my gift, because of the whiskey that makes me fluent in their corvid tongue. Its remnants burn my throat.

A storm of wings. A squawking murder of feathered intellectuals nearly crashes into me; I duck, my shoulder grazed.

One of their ilk lingers, perched upon a low-hanging branch. Its eyes are dying stars. It cocks its head.

"There is a house," it says. "Did you not hear? You did not respond."

"I've never talked to a bird."

"You comprehend us. Gratification is customary when presented information, is it not?"

"I suppose." We stare at one another. "Thank you."

The crow snaps its beak. "Heed the leaves."

It takes flight.

I scratch an itch. What the fuck does that mean, 'heed the leaves?'

I walk and the dead leaves, red leaves crunch with every violent step, like uninvited memories banished to the darkness whence they came.

Fuck you.

I snort. I chuckle. Laughter's an anchor. To what, I haven't a clue, not anymore. It's a coping method, sure, a reaction to atrocity, but lately I've found it feeding of my sanity. If laughter is the best medicine then why am I teetering at the brink of Hell?

Breathe.

I'm trying but desolate nature has other desires. The forest floor is caressed by a gust. With the red leaves, dead leaves she is made, an atrocious puppet-memory fashioned by the wind.

"Baby, I'm sorry."

Here comes the chuckle. "Fuck *you.*"

"It was my brothers. They sent you that message."

That message. Full of woe and lies. A summation of our time. A betrayal of my trust; an exploitation of my heart.

"Do you even *have* any brothers?" Question everything. "Is *this*"—I gesture at the forest, at us—"even happening or am I in a dream?"

She takes one step toward me. That corvid warning echoes through my mind. "Stop," I hiss. "What is this place? What the fuck are *you*?"

Leaves fall to nothing; all is still. Then, the wind whispers in my ear, "I am the way to the city of woe," and the forest departs, bleeding away like paint peeled from walls.

I stand in the void, at the head of a path wrought of stones. They are white like virgin snow. I walk and the red leaves fall.

In the distance stands a house.

ANOTHER ENTRY WRIT upon the skin of gods. The Sad-Man Lamentation. What is the point of such misery if all is fated to wither and rot? Self drags their quill across the parchment flesh; so many questions.

Flecks of light yet fall like snowflakes; darkness swallows suns, and the dirge of a billion wayward souls descends in a whisper like the rattling of autumn leaves, for the true sound of death is lost to the cosmic sea.

Self writes, and the narrative deviates. Ages nest in one another as if privy to the monstrousness by which they were designed. They shelter in their own atrocities and wait—for what?

Self shuts the journal and breathes of frigid air.

Here is so beautifully forlorn.

THERE IS nothing in this place, this void, save the path of stones and the distant house. I do not know if I am dreaming or awake.

"Heed the leaves."

"I am the way to the city of woe."

Cryptic corvids. Recondite whisperings of wind and leaves. Why is there always an absence of straightforwardness to these things?

The eldritch mystique of the forest surrounding my hometown picks at me like I would a scab. There is something deeper, else why would I have spent my college years engrossed in local history as I manufactured fictions of infections, wolves, and woe? What is it about the local dead that holds our sway? That called me to the cemetery past our house more times than I can count?

A temperate wind caresses me. A melody is born of the emptiness of this place. Ellie Goulding's rendition of *Hanging On* by Active Child enfolds me like a winter cloak and I am, for a moment, on that upward path toward tombstones while the clouds give way to rain.

(I have recalled that walk so many times in the years since. There is solace in things that *were* but no longer *are*.)

The reverie fades and I stand before the house. The void peels away and the forest blooms like a Rorschach test.

The leaves, still, are red.

They rattle in the breeze.

The house is two-stories tall, a converted hunting cabin reminiscent of my childhood home, sequestered in the gentle madness of the woods.

The door stands ajar.

Between it and myself, the wind gathers leaves and resurrects the puppet-memory of a whore, self-proclaimed way to the city of woe.

"'At grief so deep the tongue must wag in vain,'" she recites. "'The language of our sense and memory lacks the vocabulary of such pain.'" She smiles and its softness is a monstrous thing. "The worst is yet to come."

I do not know then how prophetic those words are. That in this moment they have dipped in ink the quill with which reality will feast of my resolve in the eleven years to come.

I ignore the puppet-memory of a girl I used to love and approach the open door. Beyond it, amalgamated memories of my childhood whisper like a dream.

I cross into 1996 and the house is empty save a kitchen table, six chairs, and a cat.

I blink and I am a boy of six, seated at the table with a pen in hand. Before me, a journal, empty and awaiting ink.

The cat sits on my lap.

Someone places a kiss atop my head. I catch my mother's reflection in the backyard door. She smiles.

Twenty-two years from this moment I am drunk with the weight of the world striving to put me in the earth.

But we are not there yet.

I am twenty three and the nightmare has only just begun.

I sit at the table and pet the cat as the symphony of nostalgia and heartache consumes me like a ship lost at sea.

How many times will Self write of sorry things? Of sorrow and its threads? Of memories and thorns? How many times must the wheel turn before the world regresses to the mean?

They stand in the orchard, tasting of the sour apples' flesh. Dry leaves sing a rattling song; they ride the downward breeze, collecting at the roots of trees like corpses piled for inhumation. Amongst them, apple cores; rot to feed the trees, rot from which a million saplings will forever sprout and in whose fruit shall sleep regret and woe and all that makes Self weep.

"What an awful place," Self murmurs. To the wind, to no one, to everyone. "What a cruelty it is, being birthed of pain."

They sit amongst the apple cores and leaves. They open the godskin journal and turn to a page yet kissed by ink.

The house of leaves and ash can wait.

It will always wait.

WOODS & THRONE
AUGUST 27, 2015, AUGUST 27, 2016

"In the dark wood do they come—Raum, wisest of them all. Noblest of thrones. They who dwell at the start and end of time."

It is midnight. It is my birthday. I have been listening to *Confessions* by Alesana for the past hour. In times of creation, when I feel my energy slipping toward the end of a project, I turn to my favorite band for that extra, metaphorical kick in the pants.

I am twenty five, now. I have written three books; I am working on my fourth. Someone once said writing a book gets easier the more you do it; clearly, they never wrote anything.

I pound my second Honey Stinger (Jack

Daniel's Tennessee Honey and Sprite for anyone who wants to make a horrible life choice) then leave the house to go for a walk. It's habitual, the walk. A melancholic exercising of the mind and body; the means to puzzle out a scene and simultaneously brood.

My invariability carries me up the street behind my house, northeast to a one-lane backroad leading to my favorite muse—the Verdugo Hills Pioneer Cemetery. Its influence on and presence in my books cannot be overlooked; it is a waypoint in my life. Here were so many characters conceived; here were they left to rot in stories incomplete.

I squeeze beyond the wrought iron gate; they chain it loosely these days. The history of this place, like so many other things in town, holds little weight. Who's going to visit the bones of pioneers when you can shotgun beer that tastes like piss or shoot up meth behind the park?

The irreverence shown the burial ground is evident. Weeds are plentiful, headstones caked in layers of dirt and bird shit. If there was once a path to navigate it's long been lost to unbounded scrub.

"Sorry," I murmur to myriad ghosts unseen. "I

wish they kept it up, but they don't. You should see the lower side of town…"

As if ghosts give a damn.

Somewhere in the trees an owl hoots.

My thoughts return to the book I'm drafting, to the scene that's got me stuck. Relative to the story as a whole it's a very trivial thing. But to the character I'm writing there is nothing else—how do I convey grief in the wake of a mother's death?

I am three years, one month, and twenty two days from being able to answer that, so I think about the early hours of January 1, 2011. All of us stuck in a hospital in a city whose name I've long repressed. Getting the voicemail of everyone I call. Having the oldest of us call his parents. Watching, listening to a parent's agony as they arrive and someone tells them in tearful Spanish that their boy is dead.

The drive home at sunrise.

Numb.

Still numb after all these years—until I'm not, and my heart feels like a wad of paper crumpled way too many times to be of use. Tossed in the bin only to be retrieved; some of it still works, you just need to look in the fissures and folds.

The bushes rustle and a raccoon comes waddling out on twos with a condom in its hand.

The rubber is *used* and tied off at the end, the way they tell you to before you throw it in the trash.

A second, smaller raccoon follows suit. "The fuck you looking at, sad boy?"

They wander off and I am not entirely sure I'm awake. I'm definitely *not* sober. I double over and retch, piling on the irreverence.

"Sorry," I murmur again.

The ghosts do not reply. Why would they?

When I have finished purging myself I straighten up. I feel weighted down by the memory of that January night. I feel... I don't know how to describe it. Like everything *is* fine but there's something lurking, leering, waiting to erupt. Like the darkness has a finger on my spine.

I need sleep, I decide, and bid the ghosts goodbye.

I am hardly two feet from the cemetery gate, when from my peripheral, I see her manifest in the northward trees, this girl of paper flesh and moonlit eyes. She meets my gaze, puts a finger to her lips, and in a twist of light, is gone.

Later that night I dream.

A town rots and a thing called Sorrow chronicles its end.

Self drags their quill across the pages of the godskin journal, chronicling the memory of a paper-thing yet made. Of paper-*things* yet trapped in the womb of fabrication. No, not trapped— asleep. Rushed creation leads to stillborn stories; they are parables in and of themselves. A chess match featuring idleness and action.

Self sets the quill aside and shuts the journal; it creaks as leathered skin so often does. Self sighs; they recline against the trunk of an apple tree. Its branches bloom; sour memories lie in wait for the tree has feasted well these several months, tasting of the compost flesh of apples past. One of many virgin oaks; a vessel for the dreams and nightmares yet conceived.

"No," Self murmurs. "We have been over this time and again." They hiss, massaging the spot between their absent eyes. "All that ever was and will be *is* for we hath made it so, else the apples would not grow."

Beautiful tumors. Veiled malignancy.

Self curls into a ball. "God or serpent?"

Only the turning of the wheel will tell.

An apple falls.

August 27, 2015

My birthday is uneventfully eventful. I write for several hours during the day save breaks for a glass or two of wine accompanied by my teasing of the dog. She is sweet. She is dumb. But like all dogs she is an anchor, and in this moment I am ignorant to the destruction of such things the coming years will bring, for the latter months of 2018 and 2022 will destroy me.

I digress.

Where was I? Right. Birthday. The traditional barbecue at my parents' house. A lot of booze. My god, I have a lot to drink, and I pass out with a smile on my face. The cold side of the pillow feels nice.

I wake to the late-night baying of our dog and the screech of an owl in the trees behind the house. I should be sleeping, should be lost in liquor dreams of far off lands and cats with thumbs, but something in the darkness of my mind is warding me from sleep.

Still dressed, shoes still on, I slip from bed and wander out into the night, *mostly* sure that I'm awake and not about to experience that scene from *Little Nemo* where the kid hears Morpheus in the kitchen and a second later is drowning in his house. What a movie…

I'm at the bottom of the driveway when she blooms. She rises from the fissured street, coalescing like a paper rose, all the while illumined by the streetlight overhead. Her eyes are moonlight and her lips are thin; her hair is flaxen of the coldest hue. Like so many of the girls of whom I write, she is garbed in a gown the color of virgin snow.

It is summer and I have never felt so cold.

Maybe it's the whiskey thrumming through me, the inebriation yet to fully fade, but she nears me and I do not wilt. The motion-sensor driveway light provides such sorry clarity; she stands before me, a thing of parchment flesh tattooed with myriad lines of prose. Poor facsimiles of Poe—my teenage hand at the stylings of a master.

The line below her neck exhumes my breath: *"Dear Alexandra, you set my heart aflame."* Her fingers brush my cheek, and in those moonlight eyes I see the fire and brimstone bones of a story six-years old, consigned to rot in the darkness of my writer's trunk.

"You cannot cage such broken things within your mind," she whispers. "You cannot dam the damned." She pulls me to her and our faces neatly touch. "Write the words; finish your story lest the ink consume your soul."

She pulls away and her cheeks are stained—the story is fading from her flesh. "O father mine, do not let the color decay. Do not subject yourself to the fate to which I'm bound."

She disintegrates, her ruin stolen by a breeze, and a sharpness manifests atop my chest and pushes inward toward my heart. I double over, gulping humid air, but the pain does not relent.

I stumble into the house, into the bathroom, and remove my shirt. My teeth are clenched, lips pulled back in a rictus as it blooms across my chest:

In the dark wood do they come—Raum, wisest of them all. Noblest of thrones. They who dwell at the start and end of time.

The mirror shifts, fluctuates; my reflection bleeds away like rivulets of paint. For a moment I can *see*. I do not know *what*, but it makes my insides squirm, that thing, that milk-white *grin*.

I blink like a rapid-fire camera.

The sun peeks through my window. My head is pounding and my body aches. My recollections are encased in fog. The absence of a nagging dream compels my hand to caress my chest.

Risen flesh. A deep moan born in stars and darkness, wrought of whiskey and a loneliness I cannot place. A thing that dwells in the blackest chamber of my mind.

That milk-white grin. That horrid moon.

I do not dream of it for eight years.

SELF IS ROUSED from nightmares by a wet nose on their cheek. It belongs to a creature long-of-snout with pointed ears and a purple tongue—a dog. Its fur is the color of sun-kissed straw; its curled tail trails to mist. A most peculiar thing for the simple fact it should not *be*—not here, at least.

"How then," Self murmurs, "did you get here?"

The dog yawns. "You left the front door ajar. Lucky you did. The forest was trying to eat me." It whimpers. "It devoured my friends."

"I am sorry…" What *door*?

The dog's ear perk up. They twitch. The crea-ture growls. "Something here precedes me." It sniffs the air. "A fresh scent, leaves and rain. Vanilla and a hint of mud."

Self stands. "Show me this door of which you speak, beast. Show me that I might close what should not be."

"I will," the dog says. "But your house must first be cleansed. This thing which came before me…it will let the poison in. It will eat your world like the forest ate my friends."

Self trembles.

"This way," the dog says.

They start for the tower.

They start for the heart.

IN MY EXPERIENCE, life's profundities manifest over time. They are not things to be hunted, they are not the Holy Grail. They will find you when the time is right.

A year passes, yet those tattooed words remain. When my twenty-sixth birthday comes they rouse in the dead of night, a silent scream that manifests as fire in my chest. My girlfriend is dead to the world in bed; she does not hear me stir. What a majestic string of curses…

I drag myself into the living room of our apartment, searching for a glass. A shot of scotch, I think. That'll douse the flames.

I believe most of us are familiar with the effect of alcohol on fire, so trust me when I say this also applies in the metaphysical sense.

Later in the morning I will awaken on the couch with an impressive headache that suggests a bit of early morning celebration. This is not case.

I recall nothing of the time between the whiskey traveling down my throat and the conjuring of my personage to a forest dark. I cannot describe it any other way, for how could I have come to this place if not invoked?

Gradually my eyes adjust; a layer of blackness peels away, compelled by the pastel brilliance of what are best described as ghost trees, for they exist in liminality, visually present but intangible.

The ticking of a metronome licks my ears. Like the sound of someone loudly chewing gum it triggers sensory overload; I gnash my teeth and scream, but the forest swallows my disdain.

"Yes, a peculiar thing about this place," a voice like a dull wind says. From the darkness manifests a black-eyed hare whose garb is best described as that of *Castlevania's* Mathias Cronqvist prior to his fall.

"What are you doing here?" it asks.

"I...don't know."

The hare approaches; it is large, head falling

just below my chest. It bears the perfume of a million ages cloaked in misery and pine. Its black eyes narrow; its silver-tipped ears arise. I am only just now privy to the scabbard hanging from its waist.

"He called you here," the hare says finally. "His mark sits in your eyes." It tilts its head. "But why…? Sad boy from the ink-bled world without…" It shrugs. "No matter. Come now. We haven't long."

We traverse the ghosts trees at a measured pace. The hare keeps several steps ahead, muttering indiscernibly as most stereotypically mad-things often do. Here the lines between the gothic and uncanny blur for Dracula has taken up the March Hare's flesh and fur.

A most peculiar thought. It keeps me company for a time, sowing seeds of fiction whilst I momentarily wonder if this liminal wood is purgatory. I hope my body looks at peace. What a way to go, half-clothed, drenched in scotch—and on my birthday, too!

You aren't dead, you stupid fuck, the smartest part of me mutters from the void. *Get your shit together and follow the Dracula hare.*

Fuck the yellow-brick road.

At length we come to a glade at the center of

which a figure sits adorned in white. It wears a mask that makes me think of marionettes and puppet-things; I shiver.

"Thank you, Elias," the figure says.

The hare bows, then departs a muttering nut.

I do not move. "Who are you?"

"Many things to many people," the figure says. "Tonight? I am Raum. I bid you welcome to this place of mine, this forest of things between. Sit before me, child. Stay a while that we might speak of terrible and wondrous things."

Reluctantly, I oblige. I sit cross-legged in silver grass whilst crickets break the silence with their myriad leg-wrought songs.

Seemingly from out of thin air, Raum procures a lute. A stark white mandolin whose body is embellished by a corvid silhouette. Raum plucks the strings with no intent, yet with each note, starlight blossoms in my mind, like neurons firing in sequence.

"You will come to learn," Raum says as though our conversation is at its end, "that life and all of its profundities are nonlinear occurrences. Truly, time is irrelevant—mostly."

That first part makes sense. The next part, that line about the irrelevancy of time…? I tilt my head. "Am I drunk?"

Raum chuckles softly. The plucking lingers. "Irrelevant in so far as everything eventually cedes to the end and start. Everything is liminal. For example, the grieving mind."

They incline their head. The marionette mask peels away my mental gauze with its lidless stare. Abner. Whore-Thing, puppet-memory wrought of leaves.

My left eye twitches.

"Grief takes the path it wants; it does not adhere to the rules of chronology," Raum says. "As with grief, so with finding self. Empires of old were built by the knowledge of failure; their designs were writ with light and echoed in stars. Thus, the irrelevancy of 'time.'"

"From the darkness come an age of light, and to the darkness is light fated to return," I say, "for without darkness there can be no light."

My mouth is dry; those words felt not my own, yet their utterance lingers on my tongue. Mechanical. I shake my head to center myself as best I can.

"Now you understand," Raum says. "I knew you would." The plucking stops. "Our moment is nearly at its end. But take heart—we shall speak of this again. In fact, we already have—"

❧

Self does not recall the last time they were in the tower. It is ruled by dust and cobwebs, by books stacked haphazardly. It reeks of stereotype.

It reeks of something *sad*.

The dog leads the way, nose to the ground. The odor drags them into the tower depths, to a wooden door inscribed with glyphs whose light has long since died. It stands ajar.

The dog bears its teeth.

Self hesitates. "What now?"

"We enter," the dog says, "and destroy what lies inside."

It pushes the door open with its nose. Self follows. The room is barren save a pastel wisp of light. Its luminescence fluctuates as if the thing is trembling. Before it stands a parchment man whose flesh is kissed with ink.

So much sorrow, Self thinks. They want to cry.

The dog growls.

The parchment man turns. "Please. I came only to…to…" He falls to his knees. "…If I do it *this way* things will change… They have to…" He sobs into his hands; ink drips from paper skin and pools about the floor. "…What have I done…?"

The wisp *pulses*. Brilliance floods the room.

When the tide recedes the man is gone—but the ink remains, an ebony pool inside which bits of parchment lie.

The dog whimpers. "I do not understand."

Neither does Self.

SELF STAYS FAR from the tower. It is nothing but a tomb of ambiguity and ink. Pain and sorrow haunt its walls in webs of black.

Self sits before the lake. The dog sits next to them. It has been…a turning of the page, Self thinks; time means nothing here. *Is* nothing.

"I still do not understand," the dog says. It glances at the tower in their wake and whines. "What was he trying to do? What did he mean?"

If I do it this way *things will change.*

The words cling to Self like a parasite.

Self thinks of the ink and the writing of stories. A man of paper flesh upon which ebony words were writ…

A thought blooms.

"My journal," Self says. "I need my journal." Where did they leave it last? "The orchard."

The godskin book lies shut beneath a tree. Around it apples lie in rot. Self plucks the journal from the grass, opens it to the string-marked page and reads:

"If I do it this way *things will change. I will kill the beast before it* is; *I will save the world from rot. I will end of cycle of decay. I have to…"*

Self swallows. They have never felt so cold. Never felt such dread beneath their flesh, writhing like a maggot freshly burst. A door has been opened and Sempiternity is no longer safe, no longer *theirs,* for fictional failures come in search of proper ends, in search of slaughter quelled by Self's prosaic hand. In search of *lies.*

"You cannot hide forever," Sempiternity moans. *"We are come to hold you to your word. We will find you, for the guilt will always call you back."*

Self looks to the dog. "Show me the door."

They run.

Sip & Wallow

Therapy is…difficult. How do you sit in a chair, in front of someone you've never met, and tell them straight-faced about the phantasmagoria you navigate on a weekly basis? About the dead cities, talking birds, and the possibility this entire fucking session *might* actually be the dream?

I have no idea, so I steer my thoughts toward something manageable. Something…real.

"I'm here," I say, "because I struggle with emotions and it makes me hurt people with my words. I don't like that."

(There *is* something else. We are not there yet.)

"And how long have you struggled with this?"

I sit for a moment, staring at the painting on the wall above my therapist's head. Swans in a lake, an ornate white frame.

"I don't know," I say. "A while. I don't mean to be…" Fuck. What's the word? "I don't mean to be difficult, I guess, it just…happens."

She scribbles on her notepad. "Can you remember moments of frustration, of dysregulation, and what triggered these feelings?"

"I need things to be a certain way," I say. "In order, I guess. I don't like messes. I don't like feeling like my time spent cleaning is being disrespected when the house is messy again two days later. I…"

I scratch my nose, fixate on the swans again. Try to breathe. Several years from now my struggles will continue to haunt me. The need for a particular order. The impulsivity. The desperate attempts to rectify a situation that did not want to be resolved.

(But we are not *there* yet, either.)

"Have you ever considered medication?" my therapist asks. "To address the dysregulation? It might help."

"No," I say. I've always been wary of that shit. "I…don't want to rely on a pill to make me feel whole. And…I'm afraid I might become addicted."

She explains that isn't likely; that's not how it works.

Reluctantly, I agree. Whatever it takes to get my head under control. Whatever it takes to be a better me.

She writes a prescription and sends it off. I pick up the medication, good old Prozac, a couple hours later and take the first pill after the pharmacist goes over the instructions with me.

Within a half an hour I can feel a difference. I feel…lighter. Happier, even. I mention it on social media, talk about with my friends.

And then I get a text message telling me I shouldn't be broadcasting that, shouldn't be telling people I'm on meds to make me functional.

The shame sets in.

I sit in bed and cry.

February 19, 2019

Today we talk about dreams. And hurtful

words. A lot, really. But mostly dreams, these mercurial things in which profundity resides.

I sit on the red couch and my therapist sits in an armchair across from me. The light is dim in a cozy kind of way; warm. I look at the painting of the swans as I speak because prolonged eye contact makes me uncomfortable.

"I have a lot of dreams," I say. "But the one that sticks out the most is one I had a couple years ago. I'm standing in the backyard of my parents' house, in the gravel between the planters. The sky is bruised with rain clouds and it's drizzling."

(I can still feel that dream even now as I write. I can smell it, can taste the warmth of the rain.)

"Thunder booms. Beyond the booming, though, in the clouds, I can hear something else, what sounds like *wings* flapping."

I spend a minute talking about thunderbirds.

"Anyway. I'm standing in the backyard, in the rain, and *it* comes soaring out of the clouds, a black- and red-feathered bird so massive as to be deceptively fast. It cries and the world shakes— and then I'm standing on a platform above Earth, looking down at several of these things, these thunderbirds.

"And then I woke up in a cold sweat, but not

the kind you get from a nightmare. It was more like…um…I don't know. Enlightenment?"

I catch her eyes momentarily, then the swans call me back. What is it about birds? Why do they fascinate me so? Such prominent figures in all my work—why?

She takes a couple minutes before responding. "Well, someone once told me that, sometimes, dreams are more than dreams."

My attention falters. I have used that very line more times than I can count when writing. For a half second I am unsure whether or not I'm awake.

"Any thoughts?" she asks, drawing me from thought.

"I…" How do I respond? "I've heard that before, too. Uh, I actually think about the idea a lot. I'm stuck in my head a lot, um…"

"How did this dream in particular make you feel?"

"Oddly hopeful?"

I'm not sure anymore. I'm sitting in a therapist's office talking about dreams and hurtful words. I'm on medication to regulate my emotions. How *can* I be sure of how I feel when I'm not even sure *what* I'm supposed to feel or am currently feeling?

(The Prozac helps but I already hate it.)

She scribbles onto her notepad.

"And how do you feel today?"

"Okay, I guess." Again, not sure. "I *think* I'm happier. I've been less irritable lately. But…" I shrug. I can't think of anything else.

We spend the remainder of the session talking about hurtful words. About my triggers. About strategies to keep myself regulated in uncomfortable situations.

Then, I leave for work.

૪ૐ

MARCH 19, 2019

TODAY WE TALK about things that bother me. Trigger me. Things that tug at me and test the limits of my patience, the behaviorally rigid thing I am.

"I like order," I say, this time staring at the floor because the sunlight is making the whites on the swan painting far too bright. (Funny thing about being color blind, the whole being extra sensitive to light.) "If something isn't lined up exactly straight I need to fix it. I need things to be clean, put away; messes irritate me. Clothing all over the floor. Untidied surfaces—clutter makes me want to scream, especially if it piles up and I've explained however many fucking times that it triggers me and—" I inhale, exhale slowly. "Sorry. Even the thought…"

She takes notes quietly. Patiently.

"Last-minute changes in plans. Especially if I've spent the entire day trying to quell my anxiety about whatever it is we're going to do. I don't do well in crowds; socializing terrifies me. It's exhausting and I've tried to explain as I best I can but sometimes I feel like she doesn't listen and is only focused on the event."

I still don't know to what extent that is true.

"It really bothers me," I continue. "No, it *especially* bothers me when I try to explain how I'm feeling, what I'm struggling with, and the response I repeatedly get is, 'You just need to push through,' or—and this is my favorite—'You need to try to not be so negative,' as if"—I flail my arms—"I can fix this shit with the flip of a switch."

My neck is tense, especially at the base of my skull, like someone stuck a tire pump in the muscles and refuses to stop inflating me.

I clench my jaw and swallow the lump in my

throat. "I know a lot of our problems are because I struggle with emotional regulation when I'm stressed or overwhelmed, but even when I'm trying my absolute best it feels like it's not enough. I feel like *I* am not enough. Like everything inside means jack shit."

I can tell the rest of the day will not be good. Sometimes you just know, especially when you struggle to let go of things, to move on and focus on something else, something better. Something healthier than misery.

"I wish I wasn't depressed all the time," I say. I'm looking at the swans now, sunlight be damned. "It really manifested in college. Those first three years were lonely. No car, rooming with a best friend who stopped talking to me halfway through our second year of school…" I sniffle. "Third year started better, then nosedived the latter half. Lost a friend, one of my best friends, a different friend, at a New Year's Eve party. We had to call his parents from the hospital and tell them their son was dead. Have you ever seen a dead body?

"After that…bad relationship. Got cheated on twice, and then she tried to kill herself when I *finally* ended things. Didn't after the first time because I was so fucking lonely living at school. Trapped pretty much; no car."

(A milk-white grin.)

I still have dreams about that year. Still wake up in pools of sweat remembering his mother's tears that night in the hospital. Fuck.

I miss you, friend. So much.

I continue aimlessly another however many minutes. Something about this room devours all concept of time. I think that's the point.

Eventually the session ends, but not before we agree to next month's topic. It'll be healthy, she tells me, and I reluctantly agree because I'm half afraid of ghosts and absolutely terrified of dredging up the imagery I tried my best to bury.

April 19, 2019

Today... Today, um...we talk about death. We talk about my mother. I knew for a month this topic was coming and I am still unprepared. How can anyone be prepared? Grief is so horrendously nonlinear.

(Four years from this date I'm struggling even more, but we are not there yet.)

"Tell me about your mother," my therapist says. "Tell me what she was like."

I know this is going to be rough; I'm already choking back the lumps in my throat as they arise. "She was kind, and she loved us—my father, my sister, and myself. She was funny. Compassionate. And..." I tense my jaw to dam the tears. "My biggest supporter, my biggest fan as a writer. And I feel..." How the fuck do I describe such immeasurable grief? "I feel like there's a black hole where my heart used to sit."

I look down at the floor. I hate eye contact and the exhumation of woe isn't helping. All I see now in the room is black encroaching from all sides. All I hear are screams arising from the center of my mind. My own? I have no idea.

I close my eyes and try to breathe, try to focus on a dream that came to me a couple months after she had passed. It's the house I grew up in, in the forest. The sunlight is gentle, mildly numbed by clouds. Birds sing. I walk to the front door and it's already half ajar. I push it open and she's sitting in the living room, drinking coffee. My first dog and our first two cats are there as well. She looks at me and smiles.

And then she's gone.

And I am sitting at a table with a pen in hand,

my notepad stained with tears because this is how the dream always ends, in liminality.

"It isn't fair," I murmur, opening my eyes. I wipe them on my sleeve and look up. This time, I maintain eye contact. "It was supposed to save her." I'm talking about the pill-form chemotherapy trial. "It was supposed to stop the reoccurrences and it fucking *gave her leukemia.*"

My therapist finishes scribbling. "I'm so sorry," she says, and nothing else. What else *can* she say that I haven't heard a thousand times?

I end the session early and call in sick.

I need to sleep.

(The milk-white grin lurks.)

June 19, 2019

It really says something about the world at large when the people who need that mental health support have the toughest time obtaining it. And when they do, it's taken away.

It's some hour of the afternoon and I am trying not to absolutely lose my shit. When I started therapy five months prior I was told I didn't have a copay, that my insurance covered it. Today, however, that is not the case because my therapist made a mistake and now I'm on the hook for three-hundred dollars-worth of sessions I can't afford.

I go to a bar and drink because what the fuck else am I going to do? Nobody in my family gives a damn about my mental health, so self-medication of the liquid sort seems a good decision.

(At least it's not the pills *she* seems so embarrassed by.)

I sip a glass of scotch and wallow, an art I will have mastered several years from now in the midst of my internal degradation. Life has a way of murdering mental equilibrium at the most inopportune of times.

I digress. I sip in the dim light of a dive bar as the sun descends and the moon alights. I wallow, aimless, shoulders tense, neck a rock. The bar is empty save the bartender and a couple of regulars. It's…calm, I suppose. In a way, a reprieve from chaos; sanctuary in the saddest way, the most stereotypical liminal space.

I sigh.

A cat emerges from behind the counter. It leaps onto the bar and approaches me; no one else seems aware of its presence.

"Are you real? Or am I drunk?" I poke the cat. "Hands to yourself, asshole."

I pull back, mildly more alert than I was a moment ago. "I'm sorry. What did Tabby say?"

"Tabby said, keep your fucking hands to yourself," the cat hisses. "Why are you drinking so much? Why are you here?"

"Because…" I hiccup. "No one…no one gives a sh-it." Probably not true. I know it's not. But right now I don't care. Another hiccup. "Puss Puss have a name?"

"He does," the cat says. "My name is Pisswhisker McKeen and I can't fucking believe it." The cat licks its asshole, all the while maintaining eye contact. "Your fault, by the way. You couldn't have thought up something a bit more regal? It's bad enough I had to walk through a forest in Hell with a satyr whose cock refused to lay low." The cat spits. "…What did I do to deserve this…?"

I'm snickering into my glass, having half-ignored the last few words and the part about me being responsible for his name. Pisswhisker McKeen? Are you fucking *kidding* me?

What a precursor to whimsical monstrosities…

"All right then, Piss Piss"—I snick-up—"If I'm here because I'm *sad* then why are *you* here? And why do you smell like ice cream?"

Pisswhisker glares. "It's a long, horrifically horny story."

I finish my scotch. "I've got plenty of time."

"Actually," the bartender say, "it's closing time."

I blink. There is no cat, no one else in the bar besides myself. I glance at the clock—almost two in the morning.

Fuck.

I pay up and leave.

The night is crisp, cold. I catch a shadow in the corner of my eye. I turn just in time to see a bushy tail vanish around the corner of the bar.

"Well?" a voice calls agitatedly. "You coming or what?"

SELF CANNOT RECALL when last they journeyed to the edge of Sempiternity. Long enough, it seems, their memories forsook its makeup, for though they dwell upon an island in a lake, there is so much more beyond the tower and the orchard.

Was. Self feels pressure in their chest. The place in which they have come to rest is an amalgam of flora-smothered stone and bones which once belonged to creatures lithe and winged. The latter yet remain, hanging crystalline and limp.

Flecks of gold pepper the sky and Sempiternity moans. Tears threaten welling; Self wipes their eyes—how has it come to this? How could *they* have let it come to this?

The dog nudges their hand with its nose. "We cannot stay long," it says. "Else we risk Sempiternity's complete decay."

Self nods.

They continue across the island, the rot more prominent the further they trek. When they reach the island's shore the sand is black and sky has bled to red with a mottling of stars. It is so perversely beautiful. It make Self want to retch.

"There," the dog says. "The door stands."

Where sand meets water looms an arch of ivory stone which bears a mantra: carcé pas lúbet. It tickles the edge of memory; Self can taste of its familiarity but knows not what it means.

Within the arch a portal blooms, inside of which flit echoes of a forest dark. Self looks at the dog. "Is this it? The forest whence you came?"

The dog nods. It trembles.

Sempiternity quakes.

"What will we find?" Self asks. "In the wood beyond? Past the trees?"

The dog whimpers. "I do not know."

Well then…

Self takes the journal and quill they have brought into their flesh. Words have power. Wherever they are going, that seems important.

The two of them walk in step to the arch's edge. "When we cross to the other side," Self says, "I will seal the door that none may enter."

Silent, they withdraw.

INTERLUDE
O, SORROW

Sorrow traverses ruined Own, collecting and remembering the dead. These parchment people who came seeking self, who longed only for their denouement. Who sought fruition of theory and were gifted nascency and violent ends by Father's pen.

I am a scream that sunders winter nights, a parent robbed of child.

I am coagulated grins on suicidal necks who could not find reprieve.

I am a husband, wife ravaged by a plague and buried 'neath the dirt.

I am the clubbed-foot boy tormented by his peers.

I am a bloodhound beaten by his master in the rain.

I am the faithful robbed of faith by those to whom they prayed.

Father, stop!

Mother, please!

O love, O light…what have I done?

Please…just breathe! O, Amity, she lies still!

'Tis so cold here in the dark. Mama…when can I come out?

Is this all there is in Own, this town of Proprium?

Are Cradle and Grave one and the same?

Act II: Liminality in Ink

Scotch & Magic

June 19, 2019

"Best thou reconcile fear lest Nascency becomes thy tomb."

There has never been a forest behind the bar. A copse of independent businesses whose paint is peeling and roofs are screaming for re-tiling, sure, but never so much as a fucking sapling.

Or so I had thought.

I trail Pisswhisker McKeen into the woods that should not be. For every four or so trees there also stands a street lamp which coats the odd dark night with dim light the color of piss. They buzz like flies and the sound makes more sense than anything else.

I cross my arms to my chest; my breath fogs in front of my face like aerosolized scotch. Pisswhisker curses my name and I wish for a scarf-wearing fawn and a box of fucking Turkish Delight.

Instead…

"Oh for Jack Fuck's sake," the cat hisses. "Didn't I leave you in the seventeenth circle of Hell with the penguins?"

My confusion is put to rest as quickly as it comes, for within a second or two I find myself staring at a satyr, lithe, with eyes like waking suns, and the biggest fucking boner I have ever seen. Holy shit on toast.

From betwixt its ass cheeks, as if by whimsically unholy magic, it procures a chocolate ice cream cone. After several licks, having found the center of the Tootsie Pop as it were, the satyr swallows it whole.

"I just *love* a good cone," it moans. "Oh! My dearest Piss Piss! What a sight for sore eyes. Lucifer's knuckle…it's all gone to rot. The forests are ash, the penguins are dead, and the Kitchen is gone. Nay—*chafed*, as if partially erased!"

Pisswhisker sits on his haunches. "Did you

shove Viagra up your ass again? What in the high holy fuck are you crying about, Whimsy Hell being *erased?*"

The satyr is weeping. Its boner twitches with every convulsion. I am four parts disgusted, a half-part amused, a quarter impressed, and a quarter fearing for whomever's loins this *thing* has ever speared.

"Um…" I rub the spot on my nose. "What is Whimsy Hell and what—sorry—*who* are you?"

"Your fault," Pisswhisker says.

"I wasn't talking to you, cat," I say. At this point it's entirely possible I'm in a whiskey dream because none of this makes any sense.

The satyr composes itself and bows. "Forgive me, Suppleness. I am Jaksov, Lord of Cream, Sixteenth Archduke of Baskin Throbin of Whimsy Hell—"

Jesus *Christ.*

"—and I am at your beck and call." It—he?—rises to full height and I am momentarily awestruck by the stature of this creature; terrified, really.

"I-I…thank you," I stammer. What kind of title is 'Suppleness'? "Um…I would really love to know where we are, where we're going, and what exactly is going on."

"I *was* going to walk you through the horniest story involving ice cream," Pisswhisker says, glaring at Jaksov, "but apparently that plan's gone to shit."

"It is as I have said," the satyr murmurs. "Whimsy Hell is little more than ruin, as if haphazardly erased by its author's hand…"

I frown. "You say that as if this…Whimsy Hell is a place in a story."

"Will be, Suppleness," Jaksov says. "Will be and *was*. All things are the beginning and the end. Genesis and history entwined."

I feel woozy. The forest shifts. Lamps blink in and out. The cold night peels away and we are standing in a leafless copse. The dirt beneath our feet is dry and cracked, the sky above a sheet of red.

Jaksov shudders.

Pisswhisker hisses. "Welcome to Whimsy Hell, I guess." His tail is a bottlebrush of fear. "What's left of it."

Cold. So very cold. Like needles drawn from ice. Self wraps their arms around their chest. Their teeth rattle, their body convulses 'neath the forest dark. The air is sickly sweet with the odor of a perfumed corpse. Things were murdered here; the poor dog whimpers.

Self turns to the door, to the portal past which motes of Sempiternity flit like hummingbirds with crippled wings. Tower. Orchard. Flecks of gold; the ashen flesh of slaughtered suns.

"How will you lock it?" the dog asks.

"*It matters not,*" the portal groans. "*The guilt will always call you back. Ink is permanent; you cannot erase what once had form.*"

The dog nudges Self with its nose. "Are you all right? Did you hear me?"

Self nods. "My apologies. I…" They breathe deep the fetid air and swallow the urge to retch. "I am thinking. I…" *Secrets are not safe*, they remind themself. "I will lock the door that none may pass, but there is a chance it's all for naught. Doing so *might* save Sempiternity, but the fiction-things will hunt us nonetheless. They will hunt *a lie.*"

"What do you mean?" the dog asks. "What lie?"

Self frowns; the truth aches. "They search for their denouement; they long for their stories' ends —but they will find nothing for nothing exists. Some tales die before their time for the fact their martyrdom will herald new ideas. Creation is so curiously cruel."

"Do they ever know?" the dog asks. "That they are fated for such use?"

"Only one," Self says. "For he was writ with the burden of truth. Sorrow, he was called, the Chronicler of Ends." They sigh. "But let us focus on our task. The door to Sempiternity must be locked."

Their chest dilates; they produce their journal and quill and turn to the portal. Self opens the journal to a blank page and sketches the portal as it stands. Around it, glyphs of binding. *"Dormire, nunc,"* they whisper. *"Dormire, nunc."*

The portal thrums, and then it is stone. A figure lithe and winged.

"And at the end our story begins," Self murmurs, closing the journal. They return their book and implement to the safety of flesh. "I do not think I shall ever be so privileged as to enter Sempiternity again.

"But come, dog," they say, turning to the forest dark. "Let us find the straightforward path that we may learn what ate your friends."

June 19, 2019—I think

We emerge from the copse, which sits atop a hill, entering a blasted land above which grey clouds strafe the rust-red sky. It makes me think of Mordor and all its dust and shadows; fear *clings* to the air and tastes of candied rot.

I retch.

Thunder crashes. The distant squawking of a murder manifests, rhythm to the thunder's lead. The song has only just begun.

"Where do we go?" I ask.

Jaksov points—with his finger, thank you—to a ruin at the bottom of our hill. "Some of us yet remain, do you see?"

I don't, my eyesight is shit, but I indulge him nonetheless. "Anyone you know?"

He shakes his head, brow knit in confusion. "I have never met a thing of parchment flesh… But perhaps they bring news."

"*Or*," Pisswhisker says, "maybe they're expecting us. Maybe they want to bleed us dry." He glares at the satyr. "Wouldn't blame them after that night at that bar in the Seventh."

I don't want to know.

I shrug. "Only one way to find out."

Pisswhisker grumbles. "I just wanted to tell a fucking story about ice cream. God damn it…"

We descend through weeds and dirt. The pathway is lined with the corpses of myriad flowers; roses, tulips, and the like. Phantom giggling serenades us; my arm hair stands on end.

We cross the broken threshold, leered at all the while by effigies beset by weathering and rot. Eyeless, yet they bore into me; I shiver.

The town they ward(ed) is a carcass; buildings bear their wooden frames like bones, their stone flesh eaten away by time. So many weeds. So many flowers, dead and dry, petals papered. If they could speak, what secrets would they spill?

We reach the square, at the center of which a fountain sits. Immediately we are beset by figures lithe, of parchment flesh and scarlet eyes.

"Who art thou from atop the hill?" one asks.

"No one, really," I say. Not by choice, mind you, but necessity. Piss is hissing at the paper-things and Jaksov's cock is trembling so horrendously as to render him mute.

Fuck.

"A lie," the second says.

Oh. Literalists. "Uh…" I massage my eyes. "Look. I can't speak for these two, but I'm inconsequential. I was drinking, then I followed this cat, then the satyr appeared, and now we're here. Couldn't tell you *why* since I don't know. Something about Whimsy Hell being erased?"

"Indeed," the first one says. "Smeared ink where once the Kitchen stood. Rot where lakes once sat. The fat of this world trimmed."

Piss stops hissing. "Trimmed for what?"

"That we might graft our dying world to thine," the second says. "For reclamation, death."

"Well, that's completely fucked," Pisswhisker says. He looks at me. "You should probably just leave."

I scowl. "And where, exactly, would I go?"

"Indeed, your egress is no more," Jaksov says, having finally subdued his cock. "I fear the straightforward path is here—wherever *here* is."

Jesus leaping Christ…

"Ok." I look at the paper-things. "You want to you save your world by whateverthefucking to this one, to Whimsy Hell. But why? How?"

The second one chuckles and it sounds like wind-tossed leaves. "Thy inquiry betrays thy novice mind. Thou art an author of a sort, so says thy inebriated breath, but were thou *skilled*, thou wouldst know—from death, life. Decomposition for the sake of composition."

Something about that gives me pause. Three

years from now I will ponder such insanity, in writing and in life. There is subtext. There is *suggestion.*

But we are not there yet.

One of the paper-things gestures to a distant wood beyond the ruin, a cloak of trees from which the color has decayed. "Be on thy way, if thou desires so. We will not bar thy curiosity. But know this—in the dark wood do they come."

Where have I heard that before…?

They go about their business, do the paper-things, leaving me to ponder nebulous profundity while cat and satyr yearn for scotch and cream of the confectionary kind.

The forest holds my gaze. From its distant darkness comes a whisper out of time. She is conjured by a breeze, this girl of memories and leaves. Whore-thing from a dark-wood dream. She extends to me her hand.

I frown. "Why should I?"

"Like I said those years ago—I am the way to the city of woe." Her voice is sharp, like the snapping of a branch. Time has not been kind; *my memory* has not been kind, for what is *she* but a simulacrum of decay? They say monstrous things are often painted gold.

Yet, I accept her hand, and with its touch the

world around me wilts, peels away like old paint stripped from walls. There is familiarity in demise, in the turning of a stillborn page.

"A strange thing," says something in the dark.

The blackness smells of earth and rain.

The girl of memories and leaves holds tight my hand; her composition *rattles*, then *departs*.

"There is such…*mystery* in gloom," the something says. "Wouldst thou not agree?"

I wait for the world to bloom.

The something chuckles. "Come now…"

The distinct scratch of pen on paper fills the air. Black-stone towers rise; they are beacons in a world of ash, above which hangs a stark-white sky. I have been here once and never at all.

The voice, *the something*, manifests—a monstrosity of flesh and parchment wed with ink. We have met once and never at all.

My fingers twitch.

The something grins. "Thy fear of Nascency endures…" As did whore-thing, it extends to me a hand; its parchment-flesh is scarred with cursive scrawl. "Else why wouldst thou be here?"

Subtext drips from every word.

"Best thou reconcile fear lest Nascency becomes thy tomb," the something says, yet proffering its hand. "Come, now. They await."

Thus, I oblige.

☙

SELF IS NOT sure how long the two of them have walked. The silence of the woods has eaten time. The trees are all the same. The only change is in the air. Yet cold, like threaded needles drawn through flesh, the rot it ferries blooms. With every footfall does the sweetness fade.

At a fork, at a white tree gnarled and old, the perfume dies. The air is pungent, now, sour like sun-baked retch. Which way, wonders Self, is right?

"Divergence," says the dog, "yet each path smells the same." It whimpers. "Death beyond, and death alone."

"It seems," Self says, "that each road leads to Hell." They linger on the word, on the sensation of its pronunciation; a soft breath cut short. "To *Dis*."

Self has not seen Dis for a hundred-thousand pages.

It is time to meet their greatest ghost of all.

They take the leftward path.

Ink & Fear

"Here, in this place before time, in the liminal womb, do ink and fear entwine. Here, in Nascency, is the beginning of the end."

There is an absence of time in this place I cannot wholly describe. A…liminality in which a thousand things that *might* have been exist as once they did before the ink ran dry.

The air smells of parchment. It *feels* like nothing; indescribably divorced from nature's sway. Yet, sweat beads on my flesh. Collects like morning dew and slowly drips.

And dies.

There are no crescendos here.

"Only failures," the something muses softly. "*Living* failures; half-life abnormalities bequeathed a nightmare where they sought a dream." Its sigh is the turning of a page. "What a monstrous thing, the winsomeness of lies…"

Winsomeness. I linger on the word; it bears significance here in this Nascent land. This place devoid of time; the beginning of the end.

What a peculiar thought…

We press through this windless place. My footfalls set the ash to air; towers crumble in my wake. The something chuckles and my heart *constricts*. The pen-scratch melody blooms and sighs. A black-stone tower dies—yet from the ruin does it rise.

"Just one more lie," the something says. "A sapling in a stagnant wood."

I have been here once and never at all, and the senselessness of such profundity keeps this place from peeling into nothingness like old paint from a wall.

We come to the utmost tower, its orthogonal entrance inculcated with the letters XXV. Roman numerals. Twenty-five—but why?

The master of this place emerges and I freeze.

"What a strange path, grief…" says marionette-masked Raum. Their chest *dilates*; from the cavity they draw their lute. "A song, perhaps, to set the mood…"

Have you ever heard the angels scream?

"DEATH BEYOND, AND DEATH ALONE."

Self lingers on the words. On death. On *Dis*. One-hundred thousand pages in the past. Their greatest ghost, the phantom of their heart. The only thing they've ever loved. The only *soul* for which they've yearned.

Something creeps inside them, a weed of memory twisting upward from abyssal roots. Self relents; the dark wood lingers, yet their heart-kept scrawl is honey painting passages of yore. The sweet days 'fore the apples' rot and massacre of suns.

A steaming kettle on a winter's night.

Laughter and a roaring hearth.

The purring of a blue-haired cat.

Peculiar things. Beauteous blooms yet quelled by frost and salted earth. Quashed, yet unrelenting in their desperation to erupt.

"There is such agony in joy."

Self's chest is tight. The dog whimpers. Rainfall sings. The forest bleeds; parchment drowns 'neath ink. From the esse of stories do they come, twisting from the darkness, encaustum-wrought with eyes like summer dusk.

"Hello, Dis."

Their eyes are anchors in the emptiness. Self keeps their gaze lest madness manifests. It roils, now, in their gut, a wild-thing waiting to erupt. At least the scent of sun-baked retch has died. *At least.* The silliest of silver linings in this place.

Dis approaches. They are something more than Self recalls. Last they met this face wore only eyes; it smiles, now, and Cornus florida arrive. Leaves breathe warmth and blossoms exhale light.

"You must be suffering to have come." They circle Self yet pay the dog no heed. With every step the darkness peels away. Recedes so that the garden of a hundred-thousand pages past might once more be. That place of sapphire suns and paper trees beneath which Self and Dis once slept a thousand sleeps.

They proffer Self their hand. "Tell me of your pain."

"Show me your true flesh and perhaps I might."

Dis frowns. "I will not. I am not some *thing* for you to shape."

(*"Hell is having me and loving only the idea."*)

Self hesitates. They want so desperately to let the floodgates break, but what point is there to speaking when a pen entrenched in flesh would let Dis *truly* feel?

(*"If this is what you want, I wish it all away."*)

"Fine, then." Dis sighs. "Nothing has changed."

Self accepts the offered hand. "...*Except every-thing.*" Their chest dilates. "Take it—that which makes me, *me*. The journal. *Please.*"

Dis indulges the request. They flip it over in their hands. "What an ugly thing." They look at Self. "Do you realize? Do you know?" To themself, "Of course you do... What monstrousness..."

The journal opens and a *thing* comes forth. A minuscule monstrosity upon whose parchment flesh are myriad scars and scrawls. Outstretched arms reach upwards like a babe; it wails for Dis and its prolonged pain strikes words from flesh. Tarnishes its ink-wrought esse until it's limp and lifeless as a corse. Dis plucks it gently from the page. Without its words, though, it is naught. It crumbles.

"*This* is all you do." Dis kneels before the dust. "Lies for the sake of momentary bliss. Nascency prolonged; a garden for your vore."

Self thinks of the parchment man, the crumpled thing in Sempiternity. *If I do it* this way *things will change.* Those words, that line writ in the pages of the journal…

They fall to their knees. They wrap their arms around themself. An old fear blooms; they are a child lost. "I am sick…" How ignorantly vague. "Something in me hangs by threads long frayed." A cold fear. "How long ago did illness tarnish page?"

"That," Dis says, "is a complicated thing. Into being I was writ, by joy and joy alone. Yet the etymology of my name suggests subtextual strife."

Pages flutter; histories whisper from the parchment of that ugly book, that thing Self calls their soul. A puzzle long quelled finally wakes.

"Rain fell over graves." Self stands and reaches for the book. "I was born of heartache on a day that smelled of mud and trees. And you of longing on a night that reeked of leaves." They take the journal into them, yet hesitate as the memory starts to fade. It lingers in that liminal space between reality and dreams. "This thing is poison."

"The sweetest things often are," Dis says. "The lie of loneliness conditions us to seek familiarity in that which weighs us down. It clings to us like caramel; we are but moths to flame."

Raindrops kiss their paper world. The suns bleed into falling stars; trees wither as the garden turns to pulp. The forest blooms and darkness cradles Self.

"Fourteen years," Dis whispers, and their voice is like a breeze. *They* are a thing, a *girl* of leaves and wind. She caresses Self and cups their cheeks. Her moonlight eyes are wet. "You need to let me go."

But how does one divest themselves of a such a thing? How do you function when your only compass was the pain?

Self clings to her in turn—but as within, so without.

"*Dormire, nunc,*" they whisper, biting back the tears. "*Dormire, nunc.*"

Silence sings in the forest dark. A wet nose nudges Self.

"What now?" the dog inquires.

("What comes after forest?")

Self's chest is tight.

("What—comes after—forest?")

A pen-scratch song annihilates the calm.

Old, familiar, a melody of memory. Of things that were and might be once again if Self can muster courage and proceed beyond the second verse.

"There is a town."

They walk.

In the deepest part of me I know there once were spires. A black-stone obelisk wood beneath a stark white sky. A campfire yet remains, an ember in the nothingness, this place before and at the end of time.

In the deepest part of me I know that something broke. A mind within a mind; a nesting doll of lies. A phantom yet remains, a modicum of own.

"Holy Christ." From the darkness manifests a thing. A cat. *The* cat. A foul-mouthed little fuck last seen beneath the rust-red Whimsy Ruin skies. His tail is bottle-brushed; he settles on my knees and glares. "If you *ever* leave me in a place like that again, I swear to God, I will shit on your pillow." He coughs up a hairball. "What the fuck happened?"

Gaps in a strange dream.

Have you ever heard the angels scream?

I look at the cat but he is little more than mist, a memory of a dream-borne dream. The blackness taunts me. *"Oh, the winsomeness of lies…"*

It comes, the something does, that atrocity of ink-wed parchment-flesh, aglow with cursive scrawl, with eyes like half-noon summer skies. It comes and sits beside me at the fire.

"Thou art thirty-two," it murmurs, looking at its hands. "Alive but drifting." The something reaches for me, cups my cheek, and agony emanates from my heart. "I cannot chronicle what yet possesses esse."

The something pulls its hand away. I gasp and gulp the darkness as the memories drag me deep. The something speaks, but I am underwater.

I fear this place will become my tomb.

❦

"The mind is its own place, and in itself can make a heaven of hell, a hell of heaven."

TIME IS a concept lost in the forest dark. Truthfully, it has meant nothing since leaving

Sempiternity. Self walks like dripping ink on parchment; aimless, waiting for the end, the destination to appear.

"Will we find what ate my friends?" the dog inquires.

The objective. The lie that gives the story legs.

"I think so," Self says. "I can feel it in my chest."

Their chest. That void where once their quill and journal slept. That liminal space between reality and dreams. They massage the knitted flesh and it twitches at their touch.

I cannot, Self thinks. *I am sorry.*

"*We need it,*" something in them moans. "*You will see. You will know.*"

Self thinks of the orchard. Of the rotted apples 'neath the trees. So sweet, their poison. Self's mouth waters. Goes dry like cotton, and the imperfections of the journal's skin are agonizingly apparent. Smooth, yet every callus snags. Clean, yet dust always clings. Divinely wrought, yet done so with the flesh of a man flayed whilst he slept.

Something in Self titters. "*Gethsemane.*" Cackles. "*O, Gethsemane. O, Parable. Anathema! Anathema!*"

("*Do you remember when the wind sang and the acorns fell?*")

The ink dries. The straightforward path is born.

(*"I miss that summer song. Would you sing it?"*)

At the bottom of a hill it sits, does ruined Own.

That Town of Proprium.

The Cradle 'neath a rust-red sky.

September ?? 2022

I am drunk at a bar. I've only been here for an hour, but the bottle seems the only comfort when your world is crashing down. The stitches in our wounds were weaker than I thought.

I want to die; the silence might be nice.

The notion lingers on the whiskey sea. Eventually it sinks; the memory of my daughters' laughter is a powerful thing, indeed. Reality stings, but I will push through to the melody of my bear cubs' joy.

"Three years…" I mumble to myself. Three years since last I sat here swallowing my pain. Three years since last a talking cat—

I frown. It's fuzzy, the memory. Or was it a

dream? Hard to tell these days. Fucking funny, really. I wrote myself through trauma; I narrated Hell. I thought that I got better, but now it's hard to tell.

The darkness in me *grins*. Milk-white.

I slug another whiskey and the night descends.

CRY & BLOOM

"I am pulling out the stitches. I am opening these old wounds in the sweetest way I know how."

There is a freedom in living alone made all the more profound by having spent the last two years living alone, together. By having been in love with the thought that you were still in love with each other.

"Stay by my side." An old card. I sift through memories of a life we couldn't save. In the years that follow I am wiser; now, though, I am bitter, burdened, bursting at the seams. All of me is screaming and my pareidolia is personifying patterns on my wall. Were I to lay in a meadow, would the long blades send me off to sleep?

(*Fucking stupid.*)

What does it say about me that my best lines only come when my heartbeat is my spirit shrieking? When the sun recedes I am so acutely aware of the monster hiding in my skin. This thing of pain, *my* pain, the aches you didn't want.

Moonlight peeks between the window shades.

The ice cream in the kitchen calls my name.

The tequila on the counter sways.

(*I thought that we would dance forever.*)

This thing inside me feeds on trauma and I don't know how to make it stop. What's the saying? No one hurts me better than I do. Those DSM-5 demons in my head, those things that make me, *me*, are angling for control.

"Stay by my side."

I chug tequila like a man trapped three days in the heat. The pint of ice cream is a wax-kissed paper shell in record time. I have unstitched old wounds in the sweetest way and I will do so many moons more 'fore the rot resumes its course.

That is the way of things in Hell.

From the darkness of my living room, it comes. Of the darkness of my living room, *it is*. I have spent so many years in lockstep with my agony I've come to see these *things* as friends.

(*I have so many friends.*)

It proffers me a hand, bisects the blackness with a grin. "Have you been waiting long?"

I eye the bottle void of joy. My liquid fiction dims the kitchen light and we are standing in a meadow on the outskirts of a hang-dead wood. Souls sway and the forest smells of cl(r)otted cream.

"Better late than never, I suppose."

"Oh, Suppleness! We thought you lost!"

When writing, when engaging with the art of lies, it is absolutely *vital* you retain whatever *things* you write. In my experience, the shittiest words so often float through purgatory before they smack the page a sixth or seventh time, the author having finally realized their intent.

(*Stay with me, or by my side, or whatever the fuck I said ten paragraphs ago.*)

Through the grass comes Piss, bottle-brushed tail yet trailing into mist. Behind him, Jaksov, nipples pitching tents. Thankfully, no ice cream is involved.

Piss hisses at my *friend*. "Get the fuck out of here."

Jaksov cocks his cock.

My *friend* sighs. "So primitively profane." It falls to ash and flees, and a fraction of me wishes I could do the same as Jaksov manifests an ice cream cone and eats it like a sword.

(*Some things never change*).

Piss glares at me. "You've got *some nerve* writing me into this fucking wood. All I wanted since the first act—*all I wanted*—was to tell a story about ice cream, but *nnnoooooo*, someone had to go and have a midlife fucking crisis. Someone had to flex their fucking ego with a pen!"

"Piss Piss, *rude*," says Jaksov. "Have you learned nothing in the pages since?"

"*How could I?*" the cat hisses. "*My existence is a cumulative couple fucking scenes!*" He settles on his haunches. *Cries…* "I have no momentum because *you*"—he thrusts a paw at me—"can't figure out how fucking sad you want to be."

Jaksov conjures creamsicles

"So either suck it up," continues Piss, "or put the story down. I'm tired of being strung along by ink." He hacks up a slick, black hairball. "We *all* are."

I narrow my eyes.

And the forest sings.

Of castles old and the night of screaming knives.

Of a house on fire and the birth of parchment lies.

"God only knows what's on the other side," the cat says softly.

"I hope it is gentle, whatever *it* is" the satyr says. He touches my shoulder. Weeps.

(*I have stood before these woods a million times. I have slept as sundered souls lament. Perhaps you may have been a puppet mine at some point in your life.*)

The hang-dead beckon.

I oblige.

❦

THERE ARE CORPSES HERE. Tomes deprived of page. Parchment people torn asunder, strewn about. Ruined Own, Town of Proprium is a placid grave above which churns a rust-red sky.

Self has been here before. Many times—so instinct says. So whispers something from the place where once that journal slept. If those poison pages were their soul, then what yet lingers 'neath their flesh?

(*"Like moths to flame, the guilt will call us back."*)

Self presses on. All of this started with an errant *fiction* entering Sempiternity in search of lies. How…paradoxical. Profane. Terminal creations who know not, that they are not, and never will be. Has that been the point to all of this? This pilgrimage to this place of pain, this cradle of cruelty?

Dis' words yet resonate: *"Do you realize? Do you know?"*

Self has *always* known. From the moment they scratched those first words into the journal, *they knew. "This is the memoir of a monster trying to wrest control."*

But comprehending the severity of your monstrousness is no easy thing when you are playing at God. When your ink-wrought simulacra take on souls their own. When you are trying to lie your way through pain because the sugar of fiction is so *fucking* sweet.

"And there it is," that something in Self whispers. *"It will crumble, now. Just watch. The facade."* It softens. *"When last did we see the setting sun?"*

Self stops. The dog is gone. They are alone.

"Or is it that we've yet to see it rise?"

Tears well. Dry leaves fall like a gentle snow.

"Consider, Self, the absence of your eyes."

Self shrieks. There is only darkness. They crawl, whimpering. They have *been* crawling for an age. Fourteen years to be exact. A…*thing* of mud and screams.

"I just wanted the pain to go away…"

"I know, my Self. I know… But we cannot live our life in lies. Not when hope *sits 'yond closed eyes. We have had the night for so long. Would you like to see the sun again?"*

"Yes."

GRIEF IS WONDROUSLY MONSTROUS. It is the implement by which we come to live in lies. That *thing* which births discordance in the melody of our hearts.

The hang-dead wood is shallow. An orchard of souls at the center of which a spire city stabs the sky like a splintered sword. Once, it was Hymn. Now, it is Rot. And I am the Farmer of Grins, returned to reap confectionery flesh for the demon in its midst.

Armed with a blade of glass, I start the long walk to the Church of Rumor.

It's harvest day.

THE STREETS of the old manufacturing district are a crude and labyrinthine display of death. I walk and the adrenaline keeps me vigilant. Corpses are displayed midst acts of sexual release. Skins are stretched and nailed to walls, drying 'neath the red sky heat. Everything smells of foulness and shit and the city is an echo chamber for distress. Distant screams swim the length of Rot, through all its various alleyways and streets, to fuck the living in the ears, to remind them *this is all that's left.*

So be it.

I stroke the hilt of my blade absentmindedly. Truthfully I'm a bit surprised to have not yet come across some monstrous obstacle of flesh and steel. Not even a Purgatorem Knight, notoriously vindictive as they are. The absence of such opposition makes my gut churn.

By the time I am through the manufacturing district I am yet to come across another living, breathing thing 'less one counts the myriad flies and maggots bursting out of rot and shit.

I start at a muffled crowing overhead. Atop a lamppost several feet away there sits a bird of feathers black with eyes like bleeding stars.

"Told you not to sneak like that, Skúl'dar," I say. "Nearly shat myself. You come to scare me or d'you find a way to flee this fucking corpse?"

"Hello to you as well you foul-mouthed little shit," the bird replies, alighting on my shoulder.

(So many birds in my dreams.)

I sigh. Roll my eyes. "Are you well, old friend?"

"Despite the city, yes," Skúl'dar says. "And yes, I *did* find an egress out of Rot, but you aren't going to like it."

"I don't like anything about this place."

(I have thought this more times than I can count.)

"Yes, but you *really* won't like this."

I cock my brow.

"A wagon leaves at nightfall," Skúl'dar says. "Headed for the pleasure town of Cess… You *know* what they do there."

I pinch the spot between my eyes. *You can stomach it*, I tell myself a dozen times, believing it less and less. Still…

"All right," I say. "I'll do it."

Skúl'dar clucks. "I shall enjoy your recollection two moons from tonight. The wagon leaves from the Crypt of Self. Don't be late, Little Shit."

With that, the bird departs.

I retch preemptively then start on my way.

GRILLIS IS sick in the head according to the other priests in the Church of Rumor. Nothing but lies. Jealous, jealous lies. Is nothing "sick" about sticking your cock in a corpse. Even better when they scream and you can feast of all their joy. Those memories of yore, the melody before the muck.

He chuckles. All right, maybe he's *a little* sick in the head, but if you don't make the initiates dress themselves in rotted flesh how is you supposed to fuck a screaming corpse?

The light of the red sky filters through the stained glass, setting the Church ablaze in glorious blood. Grillis finishes in the corpse's ass, then turns it over and penetrates the eyes. The corpse screams; Grillis finishes again and fucking *Rumor* does it feel divine.

His chest catches fire. Grillis blinks, stares down at the blade protruding from his flesh. Can feel it grinding against his bones and sundered gristle. The blade pulls out and the hole in his chest ejaculates his verve.

The last thing Grillis sees before the glass blade fucks his eyes to pulp is a man of dark-brown hair adorned in black and white.

THE CHURCH OF RUMOR is a mausoleum of intumulated slaughter when my blade is finally sheathed. I lean against the blood-caked pulpit, admiring my butchery of Rumor's deviant epigones.

In the sack at my feet sit some several dozen "pastries," flayed from and collected of my rotten crop. In this dream, for countless moons, I have harvested the nympholeptic worshipers of Rumor, and for many more I have feared the shadow of a debt unpaid. I hope, *pray*, this will finally be enough to free me of Incontinentus Rechs.

I start from the church.

ONCE WHEN I am younger a monster asks, "If I spare thee from consumption, child, what of thou save thy flesh might I partake of?" At this point it has swallowed my mother whole.

I shit myself in the presence of the beast. I have already pissed myself thrice. What answer does this thing expect of a boy just four and ten years old? What does it desire if not consumption of the world and all its sorry flesh?

The answer comes to me in another trickling of piss. "My fear."

Joy stretches across the monster's face.
I will never forget this grin.
(That milk-white thing.)

As I ascend the winding marble stairway leading to the balcony of the utmost spire in Rot, sack slung across my back, the memory of that twisted smile yet threatens me with a tiny trickle down my thigh and the lingering taste and flecks of bile on my tongue. I pretend it's bits of tangerine. Somehow this is worse.

I summit the corkscrew and start across the chamber at a trembling walk. The long carpet 'neath my feet is scarlet with a silver trim. The walls are stark white and devoid of grandiosity, in place of which are mounted several dozen lamps composed of skulls. Their size, or lack thereof, serves only to reiterate the monstrousness of the creature to which I have come to beg.

Halfway across the room I am met by an acolyte of greying skin, starved and withered to the point of sexual ambiguity and garnished only by a silver length of cord, the weight of which is nigh insufferable as demonstrated by its crooked spine and pigeoned knees. It leads me at a pace that snails would mock.

Bile churns in my gut and the taste of "tangerines" returns one-hundredfold.

As we withdraw to the terraced balcony it occurs to me I have never tasted of such purification as the chill breeze sweeping inward from the north. It is…empty, devoid of rot and woe; it gives me pause enough I momentarily forget the silhouette admiring me from the balustrade.

Then, solace fades 'neath the rousing of a grin.

I stop halfway across the balcony and the world around me momentarily dies for nothing in this instance is as prominent as Incontinentus Rechs, this ether-wrought imbiber of humanity with a predilection for internal wilt, for sorrow flavors flesh.

"Child mine," moans the grin. "Child mine, thou bear a gift…"

Child summons bile.

I drop the bag. "Pastries from the Church of Rumor, father mine. Smiles reaped 'midst carnal exultation. I peeled them slowly as thou taught."

The grin moans again. I am gifted the sensation of a climax reached and it makes me sick. Violently ill that such a monstrous thing exhumes of me such pleasure meant for gentle hands with but a single slopping sound.

Incontinentus Rechs draws the bag into the shadow of its maw, devouring the contents in a single gulp. The grin grows wider yet, engorged by memories of fear and pleasure lingering in the smiles.

"Seasoned to perfection… Your peeling gives me pleasure, child mine. How might I reward thee? Dost thou desire a brother wrought of flesh? Perhaps a girl of grins that I might ward you in your sleep?"

I have seen these *girls of grins* before. I try to make myself forget but the image of those spindly things of knitted steel and flesh are nigh as haunting as their eldritch architect.

Brothers are worse.

My gut roils. "Might…I have leave of Rot? Father mine, thou hast taught me much. For thee I have farmed a thousand grins—let me farm a thousand more beyond the city walls."

(No matter the attempt, all roads lead to Rot.)

A squelching chuckle escapes the grin. "Thou art not as clever as thee think. So sweet is the fear embedded in thy flesh and mind—why wouldst I release thee from thy bond?"

"…Father mine—"

"Thou art *mine*," the monster moans, and I can feel it feeding of my fear; my body quakes with *pleasure* and the bile comes in streams. "Farm for me a thousand more. A thousand grins and I shalt gift thee pleasure of the grandest sort.

"Go now, child mine. Go and sleep, for 'neath the moon thou shalt make love to girls of grins. Thou shalt take them onto thee and make for me new fear."

I flee. I am a mess; I am covered *in my mess*—but it matters not. Fuck bonds.

I will leave.

I will leave.

§

WHEN THE SUN sleeps and darkness falls on Rot, nothing changes but everything, for the absence of illumination casts a gentle lie across the corpse of stone and flesh. Were I a traveler from afar, ignorant of the horror festering in the bowels and streets of Rot, once Hymn, I'd think the spire city wondrous. And it is—a wondrous monstrosity.

The adrenaline of fear has governed me since fleeing Rechs. My stumbling through this city is the passing of the seasons; every footfall is a day. I wait, now, in an alleyway pervaded by the odor of dirt and shit and months-old rot. I pretend the latter is a rat.

I know it's not.

Somewhere in the center of the city screams the eighth bell of night. With it rise a thousand more, the distant agony a sign the Purgatorem Knights are on the move. They are bestial in the dark, armored fiends bereft of regulation, keeping the incontinent peace. Come daylight, Rot will be a gaping wound where once it was a putrid scab.

I creep from hiding, keeping low as I skulk across the street and 'yond a gate. The Crypt of Self sits at the center of the burial ground; I hope fate has cast at least a glance my way, that my egress from this awful place is yet to leave.

The burial ground is a pallid amalgamation of crumbling effigies and departing souls-turned-stone, discernible only by the gossamer phosphorescence of the spirits cursed to wander as they yearn for their embezzled flesh. To them, I am a ghost.

Shrieks rake the congealed sky and the city wilts 'neath the further perversion of namesake. There is nothing hymnal or divine about this symphony of slaughter.

Midst the dissonance, though, a gentle plucking rouses. As I skulk, I happen upon a hooded figure garbed in white, face concealed by that of a bloodstained marionette. It stands before a headstone, armed with a mandolin.

"Raum?"

Again, I am a ghost. The figure plucks the strings with nimble fingers, murmuring a melody in an unfamiliar tongue. A requiem, perhaps. Maybe not. Nonetheless, it conjures memories of a dream of songbirds, summer wind, and faceless things. I navigate the pallid labyrinth with hastened steps, haunted all the while by the melancholic song and specter of emaciated memory. I cannot flee fast enough.

At length the Crypt of Self comes into sight. Its threshold is a dome-roofed chapel wrought of stone. Its true color is a mystery for its polished walls and roof drink in and echo all without. Tonight, it is black. A maw before which stands an effigy of the same material. It depicts the deity Self as tall and lithe, androgynous and twice the chapel's height, with no discernible features save a mouth.

'Yond them waits a horse-drawn wagon. I am an arm's length from the effigy when the burial ground blooms with the heat of *pleasure* and I am *bequeathed* the sensation of a kiss to which I have not given my consent. I stumble; fall to my knees and retch 'til my bile is black with blood.

"Child mine… O, child mine…"

Whimpering, I push myself to stand, to behold

Incontinentus Rechs and *scream* at this physical fucking personification of amaranthine immorality until my throat is raw. I draw my glass blade and extend my arm to place its jagged length between me and the grin.

"Thou cannot leave, child mine. Not even after thou hast gifted me one-hundred thousand grins and then one million more."

"I *will* leave," I growl. "One way or another. I am not yours to sully. I am not your knife, not anymore."

The grin widens. 'Yond its teeth, in the darkness of that wretched maw, starlight screams. Viscosity spills from Rechs in *milk-white* rivulets and braids itself into a figure lithe. Its face is featureless save a mouth. Its upper extremities *throb*.

"*Lay with me.*" Its voice is wet and baritone. "*It is time to make new fear. Let me taste of you that we might bring Him forth to bathe the world in pleasure. Such sights will He bestow upon them all.*"

It lurches toward me, this *thing*, this sentient Tongue of Rechs. Long-limbed nightmare come to steal what modicum of a sliver of innocence remains.

I shriek and sprint to meet the beast. Before it has time to react I have sheathed my blade in its skull to the hilt. It slumps to the ground and spasms. I draw the blade and bring it down repeatedly; jagged glass fucks the head to pulp. By the time my bestial rage has died I am garnished with viscosity and Rechs is moaning, trying to call its herald back like a disemboweled man trying to corral the intestines spilling from his gut.

I turn, withdraw 'yond the effigy and chapel to the horse-drawn wagon. It is driven by a figure mirroring the white-masked mandolinist. They make no movement nor do they speak a word as I climb into the back of the wagon. Half a dozen figures more emerge from the chapel and join me. Bloodstained marionettes, the lot.

Again, I am a ghost, and the illusion of intangibility wrought of reticent "companions" is a beautiful and soothing thing.

One of them offers me a blanket.

I accept it.

The wagon starts, and rocks me into a deep and dreamless sleep.

THE SKY IS black with a mottling of stars when I awaken. The air is permeated by the sweet smell of rain hinted at by distant clouds. Around the wagon, trees. A nightbird sings.

I stretch. My body is heavy with the weight of sleep, of *good* sleep. Last I slept without a nightmare or a whisper from Incontinentus Rechs, I cannot recall.

The wagon rocks.

"You slept the entire day," one of the figures says. Its voice is measured, gentle. "I imagine I would have too had I escaped the walls of Rot and for the first time tasted freedom from defilement."

Defilement. I shudder. Clutch the blanket tighter. Defilement feels…generous. Tame. My eyes twitch. I swallow the urge to retch.

"Be not afraid," the figure says. "We are a ways from Rot and you are beyond the monster's reach. Its power is bound to the tower in which it dwells." The figure sighs. "Such peculiarities these amaranthine immoralities… It is one thing to read of sin. It is another entirely to gaze upon one of its many personifications. To know them in your flesh and—"

"Stop." I inhale, exhale raggedly. "Please. Fourteen years of…of…" Wet laughter in the darkest corner of my mind. "Please."

No more words are exchanged. The figure sits still and statuesque. Disquiet pervades the air, born of the bloodstained placidity that is its mask and the tiniest hint of a smile it wears.

I close my eyes.

"In the center of the forest sits a house of leaves and ash. Inside the house, his heart and lies."

I WONDER IF, perhaps, you drifted off. Did you not take my words for what they were? Did you search for meaning where there might be none? Perhaps you may have been a puppet mine at some point in your life.

I *did* say ninety-two pages prior that this story started where it ends. I *told you* that the house was full of lies. I *wanted you* to see. I *needed you* to know.

Healing isn't linear.

And grief will always be.

But you need not always fear that monster in between.

For the sake of our story, now, my story—*this* story—*pretend* it is May 16, 2025 and the world has color in my eyes despite my wandering a forest dark. As you well know, inside a house there is a lake, at the center of which an island sits. Upon it stands a spire sprouting leaves. Around the tower is an orchard bearing dreams and gentle ends for things that could not be.

Apple blossoms bloom.

Beneath them, bear cubs play.

The sun smiles.

POSTLUDE
O, SORROW

At the center of Own there stands a church. What remains of it, at least. From its buttressed walls do splay the branches of a gnarled and twisted tree. Black of limb and lime of leaf, its reaches outward like the arm of an abyssal fiend. Before it, a contorted effigy of flesh, so slender as to be malnourished, for that is the way of the wilt. No pen bleeds forever.

Sorrow clasps his hands behind his back, considering the simulacrum's quill. It sits in desiccated digits like a trophy on display. A bead of ink pools at the point; falls and marries with the flesh.

"Was thy pain too much to bear?"

A lone tear lingers in the statue's hazel eye.

"Or did the story close as thou desired?"

Sorrow plucks it from its perch and tastes of all it is.

He smiles. "For once, a gentler end."

Puzzle Pieces (Or, the Composition of Nightmares)

Poisoned Worlds (Or, Grief and Creation)

Here's the thing: grief sucks. It fucking hurts. It makes you want to scream or punch something. It makes you want to pull your hair out or bang your head against the walls.

But it's also necessary. If we bottle up the pain, how are we supposed to heal?

My life, generally, is good. But I've gone through my share of traumatic experiences, several of which shaped this book.

In January 2011, one of my best friends died. In May 2011, my ex-girlfriend attempted suicide; she later faked her death and, after I found out and we talked, asked if she could name her child after me if it was a boy.

My mother was abruptly diagnosed with leukemia in 2018 shortly after I got married. Six months after my wedding, she died.

In 2022, my marriage fell apart. I moved out in March 2023 and my mental health cratered. Even after getting myself back into shape physically, I was constantly assaulted by my mind, by the voices in my head. I doubted myself as a father and as a person. As an author.

That's the other thing about grief (and trauma)—they can massively fuck with your creativity. On multiple occasions the last few years I thought about giving up. Fuck it. I'm done. Why bother? But in those moments of doubt, of mental exhaustion, I realized why I could never actually give up writing:

Catharsis.

My catalog of published works are quite dark; most, if not all, have been directly influenced by my traumas and my self-doubt despite my 2019 debut *Vultures* having started out as a very different project. But, you write what stings your heart, I suppose. You write what you feel. Which brings me to my August 2022 novelette, *A Cup of Tea at the Mouth of Hell.*

Initially conceived as Lucifer's humorous romp through Hell in search of his missing tea kettle, it quickly and accidentally became apparent during the writing process this was going to be something more. Something different. Something intensely intimate. Humor is often a mask for pain, the absurd a metaphor. In this case, Lucifer needs a hot cup of tea to calm his nerves in order to function, but when he can't find the tool requisite for making said cup of tea…he loses the ability to function; he struggles with change.

When my mom passed, I was five years from a very late autism diagnosis. Revisiting those feelings so many years later helped to clarify a lot of what I was struggling with but also magnify it at the same time. In that sense, *A Cup of Tea at the Mouth of Hell* was and is very much a story about my unraveling.

In March 2023, I separated from my wife and moved out. I've mentioned this already, but it's important; it ties into the whole unraveling thing. Change is very difficult for someone who really fucking hates change, especially change as drastic as this. It felt like, year by year, the universe was pulling me apart, just peeling away layer after layer of familiarity—and it was scary. It's hard to function beyond necessity when you're trying to keep yourself from going insane. And when you lack the mental and physical energy to do anything more than survive, it's fucking hard to write, to conjure even a modicum of fiction.

In May 2023 I started going to the gym again, which helped a great deal mentally. In June 2023, my car took a shit and it felt like I was cursed. So, I started taking notes for what I thought would be a novel-length revision of *A Cup of Tea at the Mouth of Hell*. I explicitly elected not to set any publication standards for it, no date. Nothing. I just… needed to write, needed to feel. To unload. So I put down words here there, alternating between it and another project I had started late in 2022 during my hyper fixation on *Dark Souls* and *Elden Ring*.

And then I got stuck. I had no idea where either story was going, and the brain weasels were becoming increasingly aggressive. So, I put both stories aside and told myself I'd probably never finish them because that's just how it goes.

But then, in October 2023, I started—no, resumed—a project I had started way back in 2018—*House of Muir*, the sequel to my 2019 debut *Vultures*. (I know I'm meandering, but it's necessary.) I had been working on *Muir* on and off for several years, increasingly sure it would never be completed. By the time I stopped working on my aforementioned side projects, I was convinced

Muir would remain unfinished and that I should probably just quit writing because my stuff sold like candy corn, so what was the point?

But then, in May 2024, I finished *Muir*. On December 21, 2024, nearly 6 years after I'd started working on it, *House of Muir* was released and it felt like the fucking world had been lifted from my shoulders. When you're carrying grief and doubt for such a long time, you tend to forget what it feels like to be weightless.

Which brings me to *Liminal Monster*, the nightmarish amalgamation of personal trauma and my hyper fixation on *Elden Ring, Dark Souls, Bloodborne,* and the like. For the longest time, I had zero clue what the story was supposed to be save for the fact it was a story about me. But the funny thing about grief is that it manifests whenever it wants. It's neither malicious nor kind, just something…in between.

Liminal.

I can't pinpoint specifically when I figured out *Liminal Monster* was a story about grief. But what I can say is that, in writing it, I learned just how entwined my creativity and emotions are, for better or for worse. When I don't write, things tend to fester, as depicted in *Liminal Monster*. But when I do write, I'm able to confront the monsters; I'm able to make sense of my pain. In that respect, it's a double-edged sword. But sometimes, we need to hurt in order to feel. Sometimes pain is necessary to part the fog, as it were, and let me tell you, the last several years have felt very much like walking through fog.

But like Vessel sings in "Infinite Baths," I have fought so long to be here; I am never going back.

THE MELODY OF GRIEF (OR, THE PLAYLIST)

Music is many things. Expression. Safety.

Over the course of writing this book, I listened to a lot of songs. Some I'd never heard, many that I had.

I don't particularly know how to list them, especially as a great

portion of this "playlist" is comprised of Sleep Token. So, I suppose I'll list the songs that spoke to me, the ones that really stung the most.

In no particular order:

- *Salt* by The Devil Wears Prada
- *Twenty-Five* by The Devil Wears Prada

- *To the Key of Evergreen* by The Devil Wears Prada
- *Transit Blues* by The Devil Wears Prada
- *Afterglow* by Dayseeker
- *Without Me (acoustic)* by Dayseeker
- *Crucify Me* by Bring Me the Horizon
- *Dig It* by Bring Me the Horizon
- *Gustave* by Lorien Testard
- *Aline* by Lorien Testard
- *Same Sea* by Lights
- *Savior* by Lights
- *Lions!* by Lights
- *The Listening* by Lights
- *Eternity* by Rain City Drive
- *The Night Does Not Belong to God* by Sleep Token
- *Dark Signs* by Sleep Token
- *Give* by Sleep Token
- *Blood Sport* by Sleep Token
- *Atlantic* by Sleep Token
- *The Love You Want* by Sleep Token
- *Fall for Me* by Sleep Token
- *Descending* by Sleep Token
- *Vore* by Sleep Token
- *Ascensionism* by Sleep Token
- *Are You Really Okay* by Sleep Token
- *Take Me Back to Eden* by Sleep Token

- *Look to Windward* by Sleep Token
- *Emergence* by Sleep Token
- *Past Self* by Sleep Token
- *Dangerous* by Sleep Token
- *Caramel* by Sleep Token
- *Damocles* by Sleep Token
- *Gethsemane* by Sleep Token
- *Infinite Baths* by Sleep Token
- *Fields of Elation* by Sleep Token
- *Where Do We Go From Here* by Asking Alexandria
- *In My Blood* by Asking Alexandria
- *Dear Insanity* by Asking Alexandria
- *Pretty Venom* by All Time Low
- *Flourish* by Osatia
- *Requiem* by Alesana
- *Fake Out* by Fall Out Boy
- *Everything Ends* by Architects
- *Dying is Absolutely Safe* by Architects
- *Deep End* by Spiritbox
- *The Summit* by Spiritbox
- *Angel Eyes* by Spiritbox
- *Rage* by President

Acknowledgments

Some things linger. Grief, unfortunately, is one of those things—and some days it can be absolutely monstrous.

When I started writing this book in October 2022, it was a much different story because I was in a much different place mentally, trying to come to grips with the dissolution of my marriage. It was a tale of a thing called Sorrow chronicling the dead as he traversed the ruined city Hymn. It was a metaphor for my life. It was called *Atrocious Puppets*.

I couldn't figure out how to finish it.

I moved out in March 2023. The next several months felt like walking through molasses. Nothing was going right. In June of 2023 I was on the hook for a massive car repair bill which, thankfully, several months later, the charging station reimbursed me for. At that point though, I was at rock bottom. I was living alone, I didn't see my children everyday, and I had a car I couldn't go anywhere with.

So, walking home from the gym one night, I started taking notes. I wasn't sure for what, but I knew that I had a story taking root, and it started in a cemetery in 2011. So I wrote about a memory, about talking to a dead friend before his headstone. As I wrote, it became very apparent what this book would center around——me.

Thus, *House on Fire* was born.

And then set aside because, again, I could not for the life of me figure out how to tell the fucking story.

So, it sat for roughly a year before it became apparent it was a tale adjacent to my novelette, *A Cup of Tea at the Mouth of Hell*, a story about the trauma of losing a parent. Except this one, *Liminal Monster*, was a much more aggressive *thing*. It was the darkest parts of me, in some ways the worst parts of me, that I felt I needed to address head on.

It's a weird book, my strangest yet. It's brooding, it's funny, but it's incredibly aggressive. It's about loss and failure and creation. I hope it's something that resonates with anyone trying combat grief. It's a monstrous thing which impacts our ability to create, our ability to simply *be*, and it's important we understand we're not alone in this.

I've a handful of people to thank. People who have been with me for years, people who have come into my life more recently, and, generally speaking, people who have stuck with me despite my ups and downs. So, in no particular order: Rowena Andrews, David Walters, Zack Bowen, Aaron Cross, Nathan Hall, Tom Smith, Tom Clews, Eric Nelson, Yaroslav Barsukov, Ronnie Virdi, Michael Delaney, Rainy Boi, Ashley Brennan, Nick Borrelli, Thomas Howard Riley.

As always, thank you to everyone who has read my work and continues to do so. Thank you to the reviewers and bloggers who put so much time and effort into what they do.

Thank you to my best friends outside the writing community (Nelson, Josh, and Mike), and thank you to my family, especially my daughters, who are still too young to read my work, but put up with me regardless.

About the Author

Luke Tarzian was born in Bucharest, Romania. His parents made the extremely poor choice of adopting him less than six months into his life. As such, he's resided primarily in the United States and currently lives in California. Somehow, his twin daughters tolerate him.

Unfortunately, he can also be found online and, to the dismay of his clients, also functions as a cover artist for independent authors.